A POSSIBLE TREE

by Josephine Haskell Aldridge

illustrated by Daniel San Souci

Macmillan Publishing Company New York
Maxwell Macmillan Canada Toronto
Maxwell Macmillan International New York Oxford Singapore Sydney

TO
R. B. A.,
BECAUSE
THE
VERY
POSSIBLE,
WAS.
—J.H.A.

In memory of
Yoshiko Uchida,
a friend forever
—D.S.S.

 Macmillan Publishing Company is part of the Maxwell Communication Group of Companies. Macmillan Publishing Company, 866 Third Avenue, New York, NY 10022. Maxwell Macmillan Canada, Inc., 1200 Eglinton Avenue East, Suite 200, Don Mills, Ontario M3C 3N1. First edition. Printed in the United States of America. The text of this book is set in 18 pt. Brighton Light. The illustrations are rendered in watercolors on 140 lb. cold press paper.
10 9 8 7 6 5 4 3 2 1

Library of Congress Cataloging-in-Publication Data.
Aldridge, Josephine Haskell. A possible tree / by Josephine Haskell Aldridge ; illustrated by Daniel San Souci. — 1st ed. p. cm. Summary: A crooked fir tree keeps several animals safe from harm. ISBN 0-02-700407-4
[1. Fir—Fiction. 2. Trees—Fiction. 3. Animals—Fiction. 4. Ecology—Fiction.] I. San Souci, Daniel, ill. II. Title. PZ7.A372Po 1993 [E]—dc20
92-13704

Along the dark woods path
Joe Bracken's old coon hound
howled and yelped
and zigged past Joe,
leaped over the brook
and zagged to the same fir tree,
the same one
as always.
Joe watched with his gun ready.
The dog stopped in a patch of moonlight
and wagged his tail and scratched his neck
and lay down.
Joe turned back home.
"No use hunting with that dog,"
he said,
"that dog is no good,
no good at all."

From a top branch
the coon
watched Joe disappear
into the night
and looked at the sleeping dog below.

The fir tree tightened the circle
of its bough
around him
and made a soothing
shh shhhh shhhh sound.

Tall, straight spruce trees
grew in the woods around
the short, bushy fir
where the chased coon
and Joe Bracken's dog
rested,
trees touching each other

with branches
leading up to
pointed green spires.
Together they swayed
with the wind and
swept storms
out of the sky.

Joe Bracken's wife hung
the wet wash outside Monday mornings.
Every time, a blue jay screamed at her
from the point of a white picket,
and—every time—Mrs. Bracken
screamed back.
"You pest! Get your fine feathers
off my fence!"
She hurled the wash water
at the bird.
She always missed—
except this time!

Off went the blue jay,
dripping wet.
He didn't fly far into the woods,
only as far as the crooked tree,
where he lit
and shook himself

and preened his feathers
and rested in the curve
of a branch.
"This is a safe place,"
thought the jay,
"nothing to dodge here!"

Joe Bracken's son
had a slingshot
and a pocket full of pebbles.
He had been bothering a mother squirrel
who skittered about every day
gathering chicken feed
for her little ones.
She always shot several rounds
of ack-ack chatter
back at him,
but still the pebbles kept coming.
So one morning,
before Joe's son was up,
the squirrel scurried
to the twisted tree
and found a sound limb.
It curled around her
and around her little ones.
It grew thick needles
and provided seeds hidden
in the prickly cones
for food through the winter.

Winter was coming.
The tall trees
stiffened and crackled
as the days grew cold.
Below, the crooked fir

kept the coon,
the blue jay,
and the squirrels warm,
holding them tightly
away from harm.

Joe Bracken's hired hands
started for town
in Joe's truck.
They accidentally
bumped a fox
on the hump beyond
Sweet Fern Hollow.
The fox bounded off
on three legs
to the shelter of the forest
and hid
in the bushy bottom branches
of the crooked fir tree.
He licked his sores
and calmed his fears
and shut his eyes
and the fir tree
closed a circle of branch
around him.

Then an owl came one night
and two rabbits the next day,
and Joe Bracken's coon dog
slept regularly
in a needle nest beside the fox.

Men from the Updike Lumber Mill
came to buy some trees
from Joe Bracken's place.
Joe said, "Okay,"
so the lumbermen
went through the forest
chopping a chip out of
the straight and strong
and tall trees
they wanted to saw down,
until they reached the knotted fir.
The animals were off for the day
looking for food
so it stood alone.

Two burly woodsmen strolled up,
stopped and leaned on their axes.
"Here's a tree we *don't* want,"
the burliest said.
The other man laughed.
"Never saw the likes before," he said.
"It looks like Christmas wreaths all over."
"We should bring our wives and kids
to see this," they said.
They hurried to the old wood road
and ran home with the news.

Joe Bracken heard about it.
"I'll go over tonight," he thought,
"and look for myself."
Then his wife wanted to go,
and his son,
and his old dog's tail wagged.
They lit a lantern—
it was Christmas Eve—
and followed the flickering light
slowly down the dark woods path.
Joe Bracken's coon hound
howled and yelped
and zigged past them,
leaped over the frozen brook
and zagged under the familiar tree
and curled up
where he belonged.

Joe's lantern shone up and down
the full length of the tree.
"Look at that!"
said Joe's son softly.
The birds and animals were back
in their own wreaths.
Their eyes reflected
the lantern light.
There were the blue jay,
the coon, the squirrel family,
the owl, two rabbits,
a fox, and Joe's hound,
all framed in fir.
A few flakes of snow
floated down past
the straight trees
and sputtered
on the lantern's glass globe.

Joe's neighbors and others came.
The snow stopped
and the moon rose above them.
They looked in wonder
at the wonderful tree
and said,
"Who would believe
this was possible?"
Each word made puffs
of white breath.
"Possible" made
the biggest puff of all
and then shimmered
in the light of the moon.

Everyone laughed and called
"Merry Christmas!" and "Good-night!"
and the shining shimmering
went with them
all the way home.